How Do You Count a Dozen Ducklings?

In Seon Chae

illustrated by Seung Ha Rew

Albert Whitman & Company, Morton Grove, Illinois

Library of Congress Cataloging-in-Publication Data

Ch'ae, In-son, 1962-
[Agi ori yoltu mari nun nomu mana. English]
How do you count a dozen ducklings? / written by In Seon Chae ; illustrated by Seung Ha Rew.
p. cm.
Summary: Faced with keeping track of twelve ducklings, Mama Duck finds different ways to group them
so that they are easier to count.
ISBN-13: 978-0-8075-1718-5 (hardcover)
ISBN-10: 0-8075-1718-6 (hardcover)
[1. Ducks—Fiction. 2. Counting.] I. Yu, Sung-ha, ill. II. Title.
PZ7.C3475How 2006 [E]—dc22 2006000081

Originally published in Korea as
A Dozen Ducklings Are Too Many

Published in 2006 by Albert Whitman & Company, 6340 Oakton Street, Morton Grove, Illinois 60053-2723.
Printed in the United States of America.
10 9 8 7 6 5 4 3 2 1

The design is by Carol Gildar.

For more information about Albert Whitman & Company,
please visit our web site at www.albertwhitman.com.

How Do You Count a Dozen Ducklings?

How many eggs did Mama Duck lay?
One, two, three, four.
Five, six . . . and there were more.
Seven eggs, eight, nine, ten!
Eleven! Yikes! And twelve!
Yes, TWELVE.

Crack! Crack!
One by one, they started to hatch.

How many ducklings were in the nest?
Mama saw one, two, three, four.
Five, six . . . uh-oh—there were more.
Seven ducklings! Eight, nine, ten,
eleven! Whew! And twelve.
Wow, TWELVE.
That's *a lot* of ducklings.

Mama gathered them together for their first day out,
but a dozen little ducklings were too hard to count!
Mama thought, "Six would be better."
She had an idea.

She sorted her ducklings into short little lines
so she could count them two at a time.
Now, when Mama counted,
she only had to count to SIX. SIX times TWO.
Thank goodness!

Now the ducklings tottered along two by two.
They swam in twos and ate in twos. Six twos!
Mama took them to the pond and back.
She watched them all, and she kept track:
two, four, six, eight, ten, twelve!
That was still *a lot* of ducklings.

Mama gathered them together for their next day out
and decided six was too hard to count!
Mama thought, "Four would be better."

She sorted her ducklings in new little lines
So she could count them three at a time.
This way, when she counted,
she only had to count to FOUR. FOUR times THREE.
How clever!

Now the ducklings paddled along four by three.
They splished in threes and splashed in threes. Four threes!
Together in four threes they went for a swim,
and Mama kept a careful eye on them:
three, six, nine, twelve!
That was still *a lot* of ducklings.

Mama gathered them together for another day out.
But it seemed four was too much to count!
She thought, "Yes, *three* would be better."

She sorted the ducklings
into brand new lines
so she could count them four at a time.
This way, when she counted,
she only had to count to THREE.
THREE times FOUR.
So simple!

So the ducklings waddled along four by four.
Played in fours, quack-quacked in fours. Three fours!
In teams of three fours they swam and raced.
And Mama made sure they were all in place:
four, eight, twelve!
That was still *a lot* of ducklings.

When she gathered the ducklings
for the next day out,
Mama thought,
"Well, three is easy to count.
But wouldn't two be
even better?"

She sorted the ducklings into even longer lines
so she could count them six at a time.
This way, when she counted,
she only had to count to TWO. TWO times SIX.
Yes! Just two!

The ducklings marched along six by six,
following Mama through the weeds in two lines of six.
Two sixes!

The old wolf who lived there couldn't see very well,
but he was hungry! And what was that smell—
mmm, ducklings! How many?
He heard Mama count "One, two."
Two ducklings wasn't a lot . . .
                              but it was enough for LUNCH!

"AHA!" The hungry wolf GROWLED and leapt out,
but there were far too many ducklings to count!

Not two ducklings, not six ducklings,
but two times six—
TWELVE DUCKLINGS!
And all twelve fought back
ALL AT ONCE!

The twelve ducklings jumped on the wolf!
"Ow! Ow!" the old wolf said. "Let me go!
There are too many ducklings!"

After the old wolf ran away, Mama thought,
"A dozen ducklings may be a lot,
but they're never too many!
And I can count them all."
One, two, three, four, five, six, seven, eight, nine, ten, eleven, twelve!
Yes, TWELVE.

And who knows? Maybe there will be even more.